Bigfoot in New York City?

(A Cody Smith Mystery)

by Dorothy Francis

Cover and Inside Illustrations: William Ersland

Perfection Learning® Corporation

1000 North Second Avenue, P.O. Box 500

Logan, Iowa 51546-0500

Phone: 800-831-4190 • Fax: 712-644-2392

Paperback ISBN 0-7891-5131-6

Cover Craft® ISBN 0-7807-9265-3

Printed in the U.S.A.

5 6 PP 06 05 04

Table of Contents

1

A Plan for Fame

My name is Cody Smith. My friend, Maria Romero, and I deliver *The New York Times* in our apartment building. It's near Central Park. And the building is called *The Palace*. But it's no palace.

Our delivery service was Maria's idea. She wants to be a reporter someday. I guess selling papers is a good way to start. She usually listens to her radio headphones to catch any late-breaking news.

I like the extra money we earn delivering papers. Famous people need cash. And I plan to be famous. CODY SMITH—FAMOUS PERSON.

One day Maria and I had just finished delivering papers.

"Get your wren house, Cody," Maria said. "Let's hang it."

"Okay, okay," I told Maria. "Don't be so bossy."

Maria gets uppity because she's five days closer to being 13 than I am. She's living with us this summer while her folks are in Italy. For the year 2000, Italy is planning a Jubilee celebration. Maria's folks are helping prepare for it. They're both engineers. And they're helping stabilize the Leaning Tower of Pisa so tourists can climb it again.

Maria's parents are paying Mom to keep Maria. That's a good deal for us. Dad forgets to send support checks—a lot. And we need the money.

Spike Slovnick helped me make the wren house. He and his uncle run the elevator in our building. They both really like birds.

I punched the button. The elevator clanged from below. Maria wiped her grimy hands on her shirt because the newsprint wouldn't show. She always wears brown shirts that match her eyes.

Maria's dark hair curls, but she has a cowlick. My hair's red. And it lies flat.

The elevator stopped. And the door sounded like steelies rolling in a marble bag.

"Good afternoon, kids," Mr. Slovnick said.

I raised my chin to look Mr. Slovnick in the eye. He stands so straight he reminds me of an exclamation point. Navy blue suit. Red tie. That's his uniform. Before he retired, he used to teach seventh-grade science in Queens.

"What are you two doing today?" Mr. Slovnick asked.

"We're going to the park to hang the wren house. Can you come along?" I asked. Mom doesn't let Maria and me go to the park alone.

Mr. Slovnick looked at his watch. "Sure, I'd like to go. I'll get Spike. It's his turn to tend the elevator."

Mr. Slovnick let us out in the lobby. Then he went to his room in the basement. Spike lives down there too.

"Where's the wren house?" Maria asked. She looked among the plants in the lobby window.

Spike has a small houseplant business here at The Palace. He plant-sits for people on vacation. He's real interested in birds and plants. Mr. Slovnick encourages him a lot.

"The wren house isn't here, Cody," Maria said.

"I hid it in the vase," I answered. I hurried to the fat orange vase near the window.

I hate to hurry in the lobby. Hurrying kicks up dust from the old carpet. It grits on my teeth.

Maria flopped onto the couch. Then she popped up again. "Hard! I forgot how hard it is," she said, rubbing her backside. "Nobody sits there except Mrs. Sugarman when she needs to rest."

"I saved her life once," I said. "She was doing laundry. Right between rinse and spin, her heart began hurting. She screamed. She couldn't get the cap off her child-safe pill bottle. So I opened it—first try."

Maria gave me a half-smile. Sometimes she just humors me. Like she's not really interested. She tries to act so old, so cool. But maybe I'd told her the story before.

Just then Mr. Slovnick returned with Spike at the elevator controls. Spike's 17. His T-shirts sag. And his chinos barely reach his ankles. He slouches and frowns a lot. But Maria and I like him. He treats us okay.

We sort of envy him too. He's old enough to quit school if he wants to. I like school. But it would be fun to devote my time to finding fame. Spike's still deciding about next fall.

Mr. Slovnick walked with us to the park. People hurried along the sidewalk. Taxis honked. Buses roared by. I tried not to breathe exhaust fumes as we headed toward the park. I hate bad smells.

"Not many people here this afternoon," I said. A few kids followed their sitters. A guy played a guitar. But nobody was listening.

"Nothing like the Sunday crowds," Maria said.

I looked for the balloon vendor. But he wasn't in sight. Then I heard clip-clopping. Behind us, a horse pulled a victoria. That's an old-fashioned black carriage. The driver sat up front. He was driving a lady around the park.

"Wow!" Maria's eyes grew as round as king-size Life Savers. She was staring at the horse. "An Appaloosa, Cody. Just like on TV." Maria breathed deeply. "I like the smell of horseflesh."

I didn't think the smell was so special. Maria tries to impress me with words she learns from crossword puzzles in the newspaper.

We found an oak with a low first limb. Rough bark scraped my hands as I pulled myself up. The leaves had a fresh summer smell. But they looked as if they were dying of terminal grime.

"Okay, hand me the wren house," I said. Could they hear my voice shake? I wondered. The limb was really high.

"Take it easy," Mr. Slovnick said. "What goes up must come down. The law of gravity." He still threw around science lessons whenever he got a chance.

Spike had put a special wire on the wren house. I twisted it around a branch. Finished.

When I jumped down, my sleeve pulled up. Maria saw my Band-Aid.

"Hurt your arm?" Maria asked.

I grinned. I was glad she had asked. Secrets are more fun when you share them.

"That Band-Aid will make me famous, Maria," I said. "I plan to wear it for 100 days. Nobody else has worn the same Band-Aid a hundred days. When the *Guinness Book of World Records* people hear of it, I'll be famous overnight."

"How long have you worn it, Cody?" Mr. Slovnick asked.

"One day. So far," I answered.

"Why this thing about being famous?" Maria asked.

I wasn't about to tell. It hurts to think about it. And Maria wouldn't understand. Her dad will be back in September. Mine won't.

Dad never calls or comes to visit. I guess he doesn't like us because I'm such a loser. A zero.

But my picture in the *Guinness Book* will grab Dad's attention. Fame makes a person *somebody*. When I'm famous, Dad will be calling me every day.

"Cody, I don't think you can do it," Maria said. "Once I tried to chew the same piece of gum for a year. No way. I swallowed it in my sleep. Being famous isn't easy."

"I'm not going to give up," I said. "As long as I'm

trying, I haven't failed."

We returned to The Palace. Then we rode to the basement with Mr. Slovnick. Just for the ride. Maria sniffed. The basement always smells of mice and damp concrete. The air smells better on our tenth floor. Spike let us out of the elevator there.

It was hot in our apartment. We sat on the fire escape to wait until Mom got home. She's a plainclothes store detective.

But before Mom arrived, we heard Mrs. Sugarman in the hallway. She was sputtering.

I unlocked our door and ran to her. Mrs. Sugarman has a flour-sack figure—pudgy. She dyes her gray hair so it's blue. Weird. But it blends with the purple jumpsuit she always wears. She reminds me of a fat violet.

"Do you need help with your pill bottle, Mrs. Sugarman?" I asked.

She shook her head and gasped, "Cody, call the police!"

2

Bigfoot in Central Park?

"Why do you need the police, Mrs. Sugarman?" I asked. "Were you mugged?"

Mrs. Sugarman gasped again. "There's a monster in the park. I saw it. Call the police!" she shrieked.

"Let's call Mr. Slovnick first," I said. "Mom says never call the police unless I'm positive there's an emergency."

"A monster's emergency enough," Mrs. Sugarman said. "I've been baking cakes all day. I'd gone to the park to cool off. I sat under a pine in the Ramble, you know—the bird sanctuary. That's when I heard a crashing in the thicket."

Mrs. Sugarman's eyes got huge. I dialed Mr. Slovnick while she continued her story.

"I saw this creature. Seven feet tall! Walked on two feet like a human. Brown, coarse hair covered his body . . ." Mrs. Sugarman paused for breath.

"Except on his face," Mrs. Sugarman continued. "No hair on his face. And what a terrible smell! Foul. Like an outhouse. I know what I've seen. I've seen Bigfoot."

"Bigfoot?" I asked. Was Mrs. Sugarman crazy? Maybe she had licked the frosting off one too many spoons today.

"Yes, Bigfoot," Mrs. Sugarman said. "I've read about those monsters. They sneak around scaring people. Then they disappear before anyone can catch them."

I hated to hurt her feelings. So I didn't laugh. But I didn't call the police either. Who was going to believe Bigfoot was in Central Park?

Mr. Slovnick arrived. He had brought up Mom and

Spike in the elevator. Mom was wearing her frizzy, lemon-colored wig and a denim jumper.

Sometimes I hardly recognize her. She looks neat in real life. But Mom says store detectives must look different every day. It's the way they fool shoplifters.

Usually Mom jerks her wig off quickly. But it squashes her own hair. Makes her look like a peeled onion. Today she left the wig on since we had company.

"What's going on?" Mom looked from Mrs. Sugarman to me.

"I saw a monster in the park, Mrs. Smith. Bigfoot," Mrs. Sugarman told her.

Mom brought Mrs. Sugarman a glass of water to calm her down. "Now tell us about this monster," she said.

"I was near the Ramble," Mrs. Sugarman went on. "I was sitting on a bench."

Mrs. Sugarman loved every minute of our attention. She acted like a guest star on a talk show.

"At first I ignored the scrambling noises in the thicket," Mrs. Sugarman said. "But then they grew louder."

"Then what?" I asked. I felt like Mrs. Sugarman's straight man.

"I turned. I expected to see a person," Mrs. Sugarman said. "But no! I saw Bigfoot!"

Mom didn't sigh. But her mouth quirked like it does when she's irritated.

"Describe this creature," Mom said.

Maria and I listened to the description again. This time Bigfoot grew larger and scarier. And smellier.

"Let's call the police," Mrs. Sugarman said.

"Right," Mom said. "I doubt that you saw Bigfoot. But something scared you. Crazies roam this city. Maybe someone has costumed as Bigfoot just to frighten people."

"This Bigfoot was real," Mrs. Sugarman insisted.

Mom dialed the police. They arrived quickly. Officer O'Connor and Officer O'Rourke. O'Rourke had a black mustache that looked like a caterpillar on his lip.

"Name please?" Caterpillar asked Mom.

"Gwen Smith," Mom answered.

"Is that your real name?" the officer asked.

"Gwendolyn Smith." Mom's mouth quirked.

"It was the *Smith* part I doubted," Caterpillar said.

"Gwendolyn Smith is my real name," Mom said.

"Smith is not as common as it used to be," I said. I hate it when someone jokes about my name. "Long ago *everyone* was named Smith."

"Is that right?" Caterpillar stared at me.

"That's right," I said. "Everyone in the world was named Smith. But when a person did something bad, the other Smiths punished him. They made him change his name. There are hardly any of us Smiths left anymore."

Caterpillar didn't smile.

Mom's mouth quirked. But Caterpillar continued his questions.

After the questioning ended, Caterpillar spoke again. "Mrs. Sugarman, please come with us. Please show us exactly where you saw this . . . creature."

Mrs. Sugarman shuddered. But she nodded.

"Could Maria and I go too?" I blurted. "We'd be safe in a squad car."

Caterpillar shrugged. "I suppose it's okay. We'll cruise the area and return quickly."

"I'll go along to protect the kids," Spike said. "But I've got to run to my room first."

Mom nodded. Once Spike got back upstairs, we took off. I'd never been in a squad car before. Black and white. Lots of dents. Caterpillar had parked it right outside The Palace.

Mrs. Sugarman and Spike eased into the backseat. Maria and I squeezed in too. The officers rode up front. The squad car smelled a lot like an ashtray.

Caterpillar drove slowly in the park. Officer O'Connor flashed a spotlight into the bushes.

"The Ramble," Mrs. Sugarman pointed. "Right up ahead."

Caterpillar stopped the car. We got out. My legs

felt like carrot curls. But I acted brave. I had never been in Central Park at night.

The sky looked like a huge licorice cake frosted with a jillion stars. The soft, warm air smelled of earth and grass. I liked that smell.

It's rotten that the park isn't safe for people at night. But that's how it is.

"It's sort of muddy here," I said. My shoe slipped on damp earth.

"Maybe we'll find footprints," Spike said.

I studied the ground. "Maybe we've destroyed evidence."

"The cops would have warned us if they really thought there was evidence to destroy," Maria said.

"I think we've covered this area," Caterpillar said at last. "Nothing unusual here."

Then my flashlight beam lit something. A sunken place in the damp ground. The area was so large that I almost overlooked it. I wasn't thinking about a footprint being that big.

The cops and Spike crowded around the footprint. "Whew!" Caterpillar exclaimed. "I've never seen anything like this."

I stared at the footprint. I know a dollar bill is about 6 inches long. You could've laid three dollar bills end to end in that footprint.

Now we knew Mrs. Sugarman really had seen something terrible.

3

Reporter to the Scene

We were still crouched beside the footprint when a red VW arrived. A man approached. He carried a camera with a big lens. And I saw a notebook and a tiny tape recorder in his pocket.

"A reporter," Maria said. "How do you suppose he found out about this?"

"Dad says reporters keep one ear to the ground," I said. I spoke as if I talked to Dad a lot. "Dad worked as a *Times* reporter. So he would know."

Maria looked at me with respect. I liked that a lot. Maria's okay for a girl.

This reporter was a skinny Jack Sprat type. He wore tan slacks and a jacket with suede elbow patches. He knelt and photographed the footprint. I wondered if he had noticed that he had mud on his slacks. I could see it even in this dim light.

"Who discovered this?" he asked Caterpillar.

"The boy," Caterpillar said. "Name's Cody Smith."

The reporter stepped closer to me. "How about letting me snap your picture beside the footprint?"

Maria nudged me. "Here's your chance for fame," she whispered.

"Okay," I said, "but snap Maria and Spike too. They were beside me when I saw the print."

We squatted. We pretended to be examining the print. Jack Sprat's camera flashed. Then all I could see were yellow circles.

"Will we be in tomorrow's paper?" Maria asked.

"Could be," the reporter said. He winked. Then he turned to get Mrs. Sugarman's story. He pulled out his tape recorder.

"Not here, buddy," Caterpillar said. "Not now. We're taking these people back to The Palace. We've already spent too much time on this event."

"Could I stop by your apartment and get your story?" Jack Sprat asked Mrs. Sugarman. "I'd like to have some quotes from the person who actually saw this critter."

Mrs. Sugarman blinked real fast. She does that when she's mad. "Well, I can see that the police don't believe me," she said. "I'd hate being a laughingstock."

"I'll only print what you tell me," Jack Sprat promised. "People need to know about this. And they'll be interested. You'd be doing a public service. Look at it that way."

Mrs. Sugarman studied Jack Sprat for a moment. "All right, young man," she finally said. "Meet me at The Palace in a few minutes. Apartment 1006."

Once back home, Mrs. Sugarman invited everyone to her place for cake.

"Thanks, Mrs. Sugarman," Mom said, "but I have work to do. Cody, you and Maria may stay for 20 minutes. No longer. And no more than one piece of cake, please."

"I gotta bug off, Mrs. Sugarman," Spike said. "See ya later."

We went to Mrs. Sugarman's apartment. It's a lot like a flower garden inside. Flower prints cover her walls. Pansies. Snapdragons. Marigolds. Her carpet has roses all over it. Mom says the effect is too busy. But I like it. Maria likes it too.

But the main thing we both like is Mrs. Sugarman's

cake. She bakes special ones from her family recipes. I don't tell anyone, but once I saw her using Betty Crocker frosting mix.

"About Bigfoot," Jack Sprat said. "Exactly how did this creature look? Please just describe him in your own words."

Mrs. Sugarman ignored the question. She served me cherry cake with pink icing. "It's left over from Sally Sanford's wedding," she told me.

Mrs. Sugarman served Maria a piece of yellow cake and grinned. "Mr. Peterson's eightieth birthday was yesterday," she said. "Lemon's his favorite."

"You bake for the whole building?" Jack Sprat asked. He accepted a piece of fudge cake with white flowers on the icing.

"You might say that," Mrs. Sugarman replied. "Abie and I used to run a bakery around the corner. We had a good business before he died." She looked lost in her memories.

"About Bigfoot," Jack Sprat said, interrupting her thoughts. He set his cake aside and pulled out his notepad and pen. "Tell me everything you remember, Mrs. Sugarman. It's the details that really count. The look of him. The smell . . ."

Mrs. Sugarman began talking. The more she talked, the more she remembered. Maria poked me every time we heard something new. My ribs got tired of her poking. But I began feeling nervous.

At first I believed Mom about Bigfoot being someone's crazy stunt. But after seeing that footprint, I changed my mind. The footprint was big. It was real. And I was scared.

"This creature stood over nine feet tall," Mrs. Sugarman said. "And his hair—it was about the color of Cody's hair. A cinnamon reddish brown. Dry and coarse."

I choked on my cake. I hated having my hair compared to Bigfoot's.

"What sound did this creature make?" Jack Sprat asked. "Did you hear anything unusual?"

I leaned forward. Mrs. Sugarman hadn't mentioned a sound before.

"A grunting," she said. "Like a hog with young. When it saw me, it bellowed. Then it dashed away."

Jack Sprat jotted down Mrs. Sugarman's words. Then he took another photo of all of us.

Maria and I left after Jack Sprat. At home, Mom had supper ready.

"I think I have it figured out," Maria said as we ate. "Probably some gorilla escaped from the zoo. That's what Mrs. Sugarman must have seen. A gorilla print."

"That footprint was too big for a gorilla," I said.

"How many gorilla prints have you seen lately?" Maria asked.

I grinned. "None. Gorillas don't leave prints on concrete. But I wouldn't blame one for escaping from that crummy zoo."

Maria looked at me like she was so smart. "Those animals are protected behind bars, Cody," she said. "A gorilla would be in danger if it escaped in New York City."

"Just try to forget about the whole evening," Mom said.

After supper Mom unfolded our couch. It makes up into the bed where Maria sleeps. Maria sighed as she said good night. Mom snapped off the light.

"Mom, please wake us early tomorrow," I said. "It's Sunday." Maria and I need extra time when we deliver the Sunday paper.

I lay awake thinking about Bigfoot. He might sneak right inside our building. Could he break down doors? Maybe he could come right through walls. Or he might hide in our dank basement.

I could hardly wait for morning. I was scared. But I was also excited. Surely I would be mentioned in Jack Sprat's story.

Maria was right. I would be a little bit famous. For a while.

I fell asleep thinking about Dad. What would he think when he saw my picture in the paper? Surely he would see it. Everyone reads *The Times*. Maybe he would be so proud of me that he would call me right away.

I tried to imagine what Dad would say to me. And what would I say back to him.

4

A Visit to the Zoo

When I awakened the next morning, I had been dreaming about Bigfoot. He had been hiding in the elevator. I felt shaky.

After breakfast Maria and I hurried to Tony's Newsstand. Because the newspapers are so much heavier, we use a wagon to carry *The Sunday Times* back to The Palace.

Maria charges our customers extra for the weekend

papers. They think it's worth it to find the paper at their door.

I skipped to keep up with Maria. We could hardly wait to see Jack Sprat's article and picture.

One wagon wheel squeaked. The wagon handle clanked at the sidewalk cracks. But I didn't complain. I was too busy watching for Bigfoot. He could be anywhere.

The morning smelled clean. Like someone had scrubbed it during the night. That helped me relax. Mrs. Sugarman had said Bigfoot smelled like you-know-what.

Tony's Newsstand at the Princess Hotel is small. But we always buy our papers from him. He treats us like real businesspeople. I like his smile. I also like his blue apron with pockets that hold his change.

"Hello, bambinos," Tony said, smiling. He clipped the wire from around a bundle of papers. "Fine day, no?"

"Yeah, Tony," Maria said. She began counting papers.

I inhaled the smell of fresh newsprint. It blended with the coffee aroma coming from the snack shop. I like Sunday morning smells.

Tony checked Maria's paper count. And Maria paid for 15 copies. She held them on the wagon while I pulled the load.

I had wanted to look for the Bigfoot article. But Maria said no. She said we'd be in Tony's way. I waited because Maria's the boss of the paper business.

The trip back to The Palace went slowly. The papers kept slipping. I liked going slow, though. It was hot, and I wasn't into sweat. I kept looking over my shoulder to make sure Bigfoot wasn't following us.

In The Palace lobby, we looked through the paper. Jack Sprat's article didn't make the front page. Nor Sports. Nor Theater. Nor Arts and Leisure.

"There it is!" Maria shouted and pointed.

Rats. Maria found the article first.

I studied it carefully. "Neat picture, Maria. Really cool," I said. I felt a little closer to fame.

The caption read, "BIGFOOT IN CENTRAL PARK?" I began reading the fine print.

The article read, "A call from Mrs. Lucille Sugarman at The Palace Apartments brought police to Central Park. They searched for a monster she claimed to have seen there. Houseplant consultant and self-styled scientist George Slovnick III made a statement. 'I believe the footprint at the scene might be that of the creature known as Bigfoot.'"

I frowned. I didn't know Spike had a Roman numeral after his name. And scientist? Did he tell the reporter that?

"It's not fair for them to make fun of Spike. *Self-*

styled." I jabbed the word with my finger. "That's a trick word. Reporters use it to say one thing when they mean another. Dad told me about trick words before he moved out."

"What's so tricky about it?" Maria asked.

"Jack Sprat couldn't come right out and say Spike's a phony scientist. So he wrote *self-styled,"* I said.

I couldn't blame Jack Sprat for doubting Spike, though. Spike isn't even out of high school yet.

"Know any more trick words?" Maria asked.

I rocked on my heels as I thought. *"Earthy,"* I said. "In reporter language, an earthy person is one who swears a lot. And has a red complexion. Translation—a drunk."

Spike took us to the twelfth floor where some of our customers live. And he bought a paper from us. Usually he just picks up somebody's paper that's been thrown out.

After we finished delivering papers, we went to our apartment. We didn't blurt anything about our picture. We wanted Mom to find it on her own. We waited. And waited.

"Well!" Mom said at last. I poked Maria. I thought Mom had seen our picture.

Mom read aloud. " 'Shoplifters hit Manhattan stores. Six stores reported major thefts of jewelry and watches this past week.' " Mom read the list of stores.

"Jeepers, Mom," I said. "You work for three of them."

"Right," Mom said. "I may be fired if these thefts continue." She was wearing her concerned look.

Maria's eyes got the Life Saver look again. "You mean it's up to you to catch those guys?" she asked.

"They could be gals, you know," Mom said. "And yes. It's my job to catch them."

Then Mom spotted our picture. "You two really did make the news!" she said.

I grinned. I liked being a little bit famous.

"May Cody and I go to the park this morning and look for Bigfoot?" Maria asked.

"Sure, kids," Mom said. "But this is just someone's joke."

I was scared of going to the park. But I didn't let on to Maria. And I hated to leave the telephone. Surely Dad would see my picture and call me today.

"You two go look all you want to," Mom said. "Just follow my rules. Stay with Mr. Slovnick or Spike. And keep on the main paths."

"Let's go," Maria said to me.

I didn't want to go. But I couldn't explain to Maria or Mom about the phone. Maybe Dad hadn't seen my picture yet. He always slept late on Sundays. He might not call until later in the day.

Spike took us to the basement. Mr. Slovnick agreed to go with us to the park.

"Mr. Slovnick," I said, "Bigfoot would probably be sleeping in the daytime, wouldn't he?"

"Stands to reason," Mr. Slovnick said. "Bigfoot may very well be *nocturnal.*" The science teacher strikes again.

"We mustn't make too much noise around dark, shaded spots," Mr. Slovnick continued.

"We won't," Maria said. "I'd like to check out the zoo. I think the gorilla may have escaped. Maybe that's what Mrs. Sugarman saw."

"Spike," Mr. Slovnick said. "If we're not back in two hours, send help."

"Right." Spike nodded as we left The Palace.

I wondered if Dad would be worried if he knew I was going to hunt Bigfoot. I shrugged. Guess he didn't really care that much about me. Or he wouldn't have gone away.

Sometimes I pretend that Mr. Slovnick is my dad. And that Spike is my brother. We make a pretty good family.

"Let's see if a wren's found my birdhouse yet," I said.

"It's too soon," Maria said. "You can't expect immediate action when it comes to wrens."

"Let's check anyway," I said. I hate it when Maria

is bossy. To listen to her, you'd think she'd spent years watching wren houses.

We walked toward the oak. We passed a kid playing a recorder. People were tossing him nickels and dimes. Then we saw a Gypsy playing an accordion while his poodle danced on its hind legs. He had a nice crowd. I wondered if Bigfoot liked music.

When we reached the oak, I had to agree with Maria. It was too soon to expect a resident wren.

"Let's go to the zoo, Cody," Maria said. "Let's see if that gorilla's missing."

I held my face still. The way I always do when I disagree with Maria. And I didn't hurry toward the zoo.

By the time we reached it, I had talked myself into being calm. Sort of. I clenched my fists. And I felt my nails cut into my palms. I don't like big animals. I didn't even look as we passed the lion and tiger cages.

"Cody!" Maria cried.

Maria's voice sent a shiver down my backbone. I looked where she was looking. The gorilla cage was empty.

5

The Vanished Footprint

Maria and I rushed to the gorilla cage. But Mr. Slovnick waited on a bench. He told us he was too old to be a detective.

Sure enough! The cage door stood open a crack.

I hated the yucky animal smell. It was a sort of yellow-green stink. It tasted like old socks. I hated to think of such air inside my lungs.

"Let's find a worker," Maria said. "People could be in danger from that gorilla right in broad daylight."

Had anyone ever seen *narrow* daylight? I wondered. But there was no time to think about that.

Maria pulled me toward a worker. A string bean of a man wearing green coveralls. He was sweeping around the gorilla cage.

Didn't he notice the gorilla was gone? Someone had shoved the old piano box the ape plays with against the back cage wall.

"Mister," Maria began, "we can help you find your gorilla. Mrs. Sugarman saw it yesterday near the Ramble."

String Bean looked up and laughed. "Sugarman. The dame who thought she saw Bigfoot? Read about her this morning. But she didn't see our gorilla. The big ape's on loan to the Bronx Zoo."

Maria's shoulders slumped. I felt sorry for her. It's hard to be wrong. Maybe someday scientists will find a cure for being wrong. A pill or something. But Maria recovered quickly.

"Come on, Cody," Maria said. "Now we can look forward to finding the real thing."

It's terrible to be scared. Even in a crowd. So I hid my fear from Maria. Was she hiding fear too?

"Let's walk to the Ramble, Maria," I said. "I want to see that footprint in the daylight."

Mr. Slovnick came with us. It was a long walk.

32

Kids crowded the park. Maria ducked a volleyball. I almost got hit by a remote-control plane gone wild. We watched sunbathers. Their bright towels looked like a patchwork quilt on the hillside.

It was scary being close to so many strangers. Even with Mr. Slovnick along. And what if Bigfoot was mixing with the crowd? Or what if he was in the thicket ready to pounce? I tried to forget my fear. Instead, I listened to what people were saying.

"There couldn't be a Bigfoot in Central Park," one voice shouted.

"Says who?" another voice asked. "That old lady saw him."

"She was probably on something," a third voice replied.

That made me mad. Mrs. Sugarman's a nice lady. She's probably never been on anything stronger than cake frosting in all her life. But I kept quiet.

I wondered why nobody recognized Maria and me. Maybe it takes more than a newspaper picture to make a person famous. Had Dad seen my picture?

We looked a long time. But we didn't find the footprint. At last Mr. Slovnick said we had to go.

Mom and I usually go to the museum on Sunday. Mom and I belong to a bird-watchers group that meets on Sunday afternoons. I like that a lot. It's fun to learn about all the different birds that are around. Even in the city.

But today I hated to leave the telephone and Maria.

Maria doesn't like museums. She has a point. If Bigfoot went to the Natural History Museum, he could hide out real easy.

"Cody," Maria said after we got home. "I have an idea."

I leaned close to listen. But Mom came into the room.

"You two come on now," Mom said. "It's lunchtime. And I have plans for the afternoon."

I didn't want any lunch. I wanted to hear Maria's idea. But we had no private time.

Mom and I went to the museum. The bird-watchers group was interesting. We learned about the red-eyed vireo. It lives in open woodlands in almost any area that has broadleaf trees. I decided I would look for it next time I was in Central Park.

We also learned that the group might be discontinued. There weren't enough leaders to take the group on its field trips. Some leaders had to quit because of new work schedules. I didn't want to think about that now. Bigfoot took up too much room in my mind to think about much else.

Mom and I returned home. Then Maria and I fixed supper—grilled cheese sandwiches and apples. After that we played cards until bedtime.

The next morning we hurried through our chores. Then we ran to the elevator to see Mr. Slovnick.

"I've got an idea!" we both shouted at once.

"Going to tell me about them?" Mr. Slovnick asked. Today he wore a red bow tie. He looked as if he might be going somewhere to give a lecture.

"Ladies first," Mr. Slovnick said to Maria. A light flashed on. Mr. Slovnick took us to floor 15. Maria talked all the way up.

"We could make a good thing out of Bigfoot if we could find him," Maria said.

"A *good thing* in what way?" Mr. Slovnick asked. "Finding a real Bigfoot could be dangerous."

Maria stopped talking when a lady got on at floor 15. She smelled like talcum powder. That's an okay smell early in the morning. It's a whole lot better than stale perfume and cigar smoke. I breathed in the smell all the way down to the lobby.

Once the woman left, Maria began talking again. "We need to find Bigfoot sleeping. Then we'll snap his picture," she said.

I gasped. "That was my idea too, Maria!" I exclaimed. "Exactly my idea. And I have a camera."

Just then seven lights flashed on at the same time.

"Let's get off the elevator," Maria said. "We can't talk in front of strangers." We stepped into the lobby and sat on the couch.

"I think it's strange we both had the same idea," I said.

"Maybe not," Maria said. She offered me a

cinnamon ball. "We both need a picture of Bigfoot. If I'm going to be a reporter, I need to get going. A picture of Bigfoot would be a great start."

"Right," I said. "If Bigfoot's a hoax, we'll make headlines. If Bigfoot's real, we're sure to make the *Guinness Book*. A picture could make me famous."

"Cody, did your Band-Aid come off?"

"No. Why?" I asked.

"So take it off," Maria said.

"No way," I said. "I'll wear it in case the picture taking doesn't work out."

"Bad thinking," Maria said. She was frowning. "If you don't really believe a thing will succeed, it won't. It has something to do with negative thinking."

Maria gave me little choice. She watched while I pulled the tape loose. I wadded the bandage. Then I threw it into the orange vase. I sighed. Three days of Band-Aid wearing lost forever.

After 9:00 almost everyone had gone to work. Maria and I could talk to Mr. Slovnick again.

"Let's go down to my place," Mr. Slovnick said. "I have some articles and books on Bigfoot. Might give you some ideas."

Hardly anybody rides to the basement. The Slovnicks live here free in exchange for operating the elevator. I peered into all the dark corners. The light flickered. And I smelled that dank smell that never goes away. I imagined spiders, webs, and thousand-legged bugs in the corners.

Maria and I stayed in the elevator while Mr. Slovnick went to his apartment. He returned in a jiffy.

"Let's go to the lobby, kids," Mr. Slovnick said. "We'll look through these articles. My science classes always liked to discuss Bigfoot."

We looked through Mr. Slovnick's books while he talked. I think he pretended we were his students. He loved teaching. But the stress of the job had gotten to him. That's why he decided to retire and work for The Palace.

"It's no wonder that no one believes Mrs. Sugarman," Mr. Slovnick said. "Bigfoot, or *Sasquatch,* sightings have most often been reported in the mountains of California, Oregon, and Washington. A long way from here."

"Does everyone describe Bigfoot the same way?" I asked. I pretended to be in Mr. Slovnick's class, for his sake. I almost raised my hand to ask the question.

"Pretty similar," Mr. Slovnick said. "Most of them say he is between 7 and 10 feet tall. And that he weighs more than 500 pounds."

I swallowed hard when Mr. Slovnick described Bigfoot's size.

Mr. Slovnick continued his lesson. "In 1967 a photographer filmed a short movie of what he claimed was Bigfoot. But scientists can't prove it," he said.

By the time we finished talking to Mr. Slovnick, we had thought of several places to search. I got my camera. Maria got her radio. Back in the lobby, Spike was ready to start his work shift.

"Spike, why don't you go with the kids today?" Mr. Slovnick asked. "It'll do you good to get outside."

"Sure you don't mind?" Spike asked. But he was already turning toward the door. I knew Spike's heart wasn't really into elevator operating. We left The Palace before Mr. Slovnick could change his mind.

We entered the park and headed for the Ramble. I didn't want Maria and Spike to notice. But I was scared. Really scared. I hated the idea of poking into dark places. Especially for a 500-pound creature.

But Spike didn't seem nervous. So I tried to act brave.

"There's no point in looking around the Ramble," I said. "Been too much activity there."

"How about the lake?" Maria asked. "Maybe Bigfoot dug a cave into the shoreline. Ground's bound to be damp near the water."

At the lake I smelled fish odor all around us. A boat with a blue sail bobbed in the bright sunshine. I relaxed. Bigfoot would hate so much light.

"Cody, we need to check out that thicket near the Ramble," Maria said. "It's the logical place to look. There might be a hollow oak where Bigfoot could hide."

"Good thinking, Maria," I said. A hollow tree! Sometimes Maria really is smart.

Then my stomach turned. I didn't want to poke around in any hollow tree. Why had I yanked my Band-Aid off? My arm felt cold without it. Now I had to hunt Bigfoot whether I wanted to or not. I stalled for time.

"Maria, let's look under this bridge that goes across the lake," I said.

"It's pretty light there," Maria said. "But I suppose we should look while we're here."

I led the way through bluegrass and foxtail that grew under the bridge. I picked up a stick and made a show of pushing the weeds aside.

"We're wasting time, Cody. We can see there's no Bigfoot here," Maria said.

I stalled for more time. "Let's look where the bridge almost touches the ground. It's dark back in that crack."

Maria and Spike ran ahead of me. They looked, then turned back. "Nothing there, Cody," Spike said. "Let's head for the Ramble."

"I want to see for myself," I said. I walked slowly to the place where Maria and Spike had just looked. Then I saw it. Not Bigfoot, of course. But something almost as good.

6

A Trip Across Town

"Look at this tuft of hair, Maria," I said. "Maybe Bigfoot's been here." I looked around quickly, making sure Bigfoot wasn't near.

Maria ran to me. "You're right, Cody. It's cinnamon-colored and coarse. Just like Mrs. Sugarman said. Let's show it to Spike."

"I'll put it in my pocket," I said. "Your hands are sweaty. Spike won't be able to tell anything about sweaty hair." Maria wiped her hands on her jeans. And we ran to Spike.

Spike straightened up as Maria blurted our news. I didn't mind Maria telling it. As long as I got to show it.

I laid the hair in his hand. Some of it stuck to my fingers. I hoped Maria didn't notice that my hand was sweaty too.

"I don't know what to think," Spike said. "Let's go back to The Palace and show the hair to Mrs. Sugarman."

So we hiked home. Mr. Slovnick took us to Mrs. Sugarman's floor. She opened her door quickly. I knew she had peeked through her peephole first.

"Hello, kids," Mrs. Sugarman said. "Be quick. I have a cake in the oven. Got to keep an eye on it."

"We found this hair under a park bridge," I said. "Do you think it's Bigfoot hair?"

"Why, I do declare!" Mrs. Sugarman said. She touched the hair. "It's the exact color of that critter. I think you've found where that critter has been."

"We need to find where he *is*," Maria said. "We're going to take his picture."

The timer on Mrs. Sugarman's oven dinged. "Got to go, kids," she said. "I'm busy." She shooed us out and closed her door.

We got back in the elevator. Mr. Slovnick spoke up. "Why not take this hair to the newspaper? If you get a reporter interested, he may find Bigfoot for you," he said.

"Jack Sprat," I said. "Maybe he'll help us."

I wanted to go to the newspaper because Dad used to work there. I wondered if he still did. Probably not. Surely he would have called me after seeing my picture.

Mr. Slovnick took us to the lobby. "The newspaper's a long way from here, though," he said.

"I'll go with them," Spike offered. "I've got a few bus tokens."

Spike, Maria, and I caught the bus to 43rd Street. Even then we had several crosstown blocks to walk. Crosstown blocks are twice as long as uptown-downtown blocks. But I didn't mind. It was like walking through a concrete tunnel. The buildings are so tall. We passed a lot of business offices before we reached the building that houses *The New York Times.*

Spike opened the door. Our footsteps echoed as our shoes scraped the bare floor.

"I'll talk to the security guard," I said. I felt important. I'd found the hair.

I'd been in this building before. I looked around. But I didn't see my dad.

I walked to the guard's desk. I eyed his black uniform with its gold buttons. He looked like a general.

"We'd like to see Mac MacDougal," I said, remembering Jack Sprat's real name.

"Your name, please." The General pulled out a form to be signed.

"Cody Smith," I answered.

The security guard smiled. "That your real name?" he asked.

"Yes," I said. "A long time ago everyone was named Smith, but . . ."

"Not now, Cody." Maria poked me.

"What do you want to see MacDougal about?" The General asked.

"We've got a scoop for him," I said.

We waited on a hard bench while many people came and went. We watched as The General checked names and IDs. He was careful about who he let on the elevator.

"Well, if it isn't Maria, Cody, and Spike," a man said.

Jack Sprat surprised us. He came up behind us so softly. I suppose that's part of a reporter's training.

Today he wore a tan suit and a white turtleneck. His red hair and freckles looked good on him. I showed him our Bigfoot hair. And we told our tale.

"This could make a good story," Jack Sprat said. "But to really find out about the hair, take it to the police. They'll analyze it."

"Would they really do that for us?" I asked.

"If I call them, they might," Jack Sprat said. "I'll do that. It could mean another story for me."

7

View from a Piano Box

Maria and I froze. It was the day after we had visited Jack Sprat. And Maria had talked me into checking out the thicket. We were waiting for the lab report on the hair to come back.

Now we heard voices.

We hoped the voices would go on past us. But no. They grew louder. Soon we heard willow branches swishing. Then twigs crunched like potato chips. My hands felt hot and clammy.

"Let's hide, Maria," I said.

"You squeeze into that hollow tree," Maria said. "I'll find someplace else."

"No way," I whispered. "Bigfoot might have been in that hole. And he might come back."

We inched deeper into the thicket. It felt damp. It smelled like the leaf mold Mom buys for her houseplants. My heart was a tom-tom. I held my breath.

"You sure this is the place?" The voice sounded prickly as a cactus.

"Stop worrying," an oily voice replied. "It's gotta be that big tree."

Feet crunched in the brush closer to us. I tried to see who they belonged to. But I couldn't.

"See there. Jeb was right," Cactus Voice said. "There's a big hole in the trunk. Stash the loot and let's split. Jeb'll pick it up later."

The other person didn't answer. Soon we heard the guys leave. We didn't move for a long time.

At last Maria raised up and looked around.

"All clear, Cody," Maria said. "Let's see what those guys left in the tree."

"Maria!" I said. "What if I'd hidden in that tree!"

"But you didn't," Maria said. "You were too smart for that."

Too scared for that, I thought. But I didn't say it. Maria eased toward the tree.

"There's a package in there, Cody," Maria said.

I stared into the hole for a long time. Finally I reached in and picked up the package. Maria grabbed it from me. Bossy!

It was small and oblong. Rubber bands held a blue plastic wrapping in place. I tried to grab it back. But Maria dropped it. She backed off like it had shocked her.

"Don't touch it, Cody," Maria said. "It ticks. I think it's a bomb."

"No way," I told Maria. "Use your head. Cactus Voice said someone would pick it up. Nobody would be coming to pick up a bomb."

Maria sighed. "Guess you're right," she said. "But it does tick."

"Let's open it," I said.

We found a red cardboard box under the wrapping. Inside the box, we found a lot of cotton. Under that, we found one dozen men's wristwatches. They were gold with black straps. Some of them ticked.

"Wow!" I shouted. "These must be the stolen watches Mom read about. We've got to get these watches to her, Maria. She'll know what to do."

"Where's she working?" Maria asked.

"I can't contact her at her job," I said. "Might ruin her detective disguise. We'll give them to her tonight after work."

We wrapped the package again. Then we pushed our way from the thicket.

"Hey! What you kids got there?" a voice yelled.

Cactus Voice. We were in deep trouble. He was a big kid. Like a football linebacker.

"Run!" Maria shouted.

I ran. I tucked the box under my arm. And I didn't look back.

If Cactus Voice was gaining on us, I would hear his feet pounding. I didn't hear any pounding. Yet.

"Head for that crowd!" Maria shouted.

A crowd had gathered around a man standing on a box. He was waving his arms and giving a speech. We ran up. People moved aside to let us pass. Then the crowd closed behind us, hiding us.

"I think we lost him," Maria said.

"Let's head for that exit." I nodded toward an exit onto Fifth Avenue. "We might find a cop to help us."

We hadn't gone far when I glanced over my shoulder. Cactus Voice was chasing us again.

"Run, Maria!" I yelled.

We ran at full speed. Then I saw a victoria stopped right ahead of us. The driver was clucking to his horse while a man approached a balloon vendor.

A dark-haired woman waited in the carriage. She was watching the balloon man. She reminded me of Snow White.

"Run for the carriage, Maria!" I shouted.

I reached the victoria first. I scrambled aboard. And I pulled Maria after me. We both crouched at Snow White's feet.

As she started to speak, her Prince Charming returned with two balloons. He motioned the driver ahead as he swung aboard.

47

"Wait!" Snow White cried. "Stop! What's the meaning of this?"

"I'm sick!" I clutched my side. "Appendicitis! I can't walk another step."

"But I saw you running," Snow White said.

"He has to run to kill the pain," Maria said.

"Driver!" Prince Charming shouted. "Stop this carriage. These kids are stowaways."

The horse had been running away. But the driver got it under control. Those carriage horses have seen better days. None of them has much pizzazz left.

The driver stopped the victoria. Maria slid out. And I followed her.

"Let them go," Snow White said. "They're just kids. It was just a prank."

We stopped to look around and catch our breath. Then I saw Cactus Voice in the distance. He was looking for us. But he hadn't spotted us yet.

"Let's run for the zoo!" I said.

We ran. When we reached the zoo, we beelined for the gorilla cage. Its door still hung open. We jumped over a low fence. Then we stepped into the cage.

"Duck into the piano box, Maria," I said. "Nobody can see us in there."

We ducked into the box. Luckily, its open side still faced a wall. Safe! We lay down to rest.

"Here's a crack we can peek through," Maria said.

"Do you see Cactus Voice?" I asked. Maria didn't

answer me. So I found my own crack. Lots of people crowded the zoo. Little kids with nurses. Older kids in groups. Touristy-looking people.

I looked a long time before I saw Cactus Voice. Damp spots stained his blue tank top. His shoulders glistened with sweat. I poked Maria.

"He's here," I said. "What are we going to do?"

"Stay hidden," Maria said. "He'll leave when he doesn't find us."

Maria leaned in one corner of the piano box. I leaned in another corner. The box smelled more like ape than piano.

"Quit squirming," Maria said. "Someone might see the box jiggling."

She was right. I had to be quiet—or else. I stretched out in the box. I used the watches for a pillow. I tried not to think of the gorilla lying in this same place.

"Do gorillas have fleas, Maria?" I asked.

"How do I know? I'm not an expert on gorillas," Maria said.

"I sort of itch," I replied.

Maria sighed. "Well, scratch easy. Don't wiggle the box."

I scratched easy. A fly was crawling on the wall. I watched it until my eyes got tired. The next thing I knew, someone was shaking me awake.

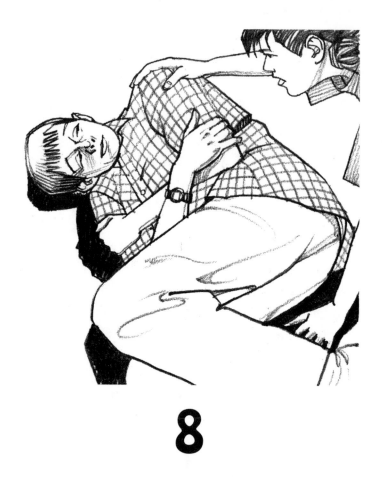

8

The Disguise

"Cody! Wake up!" Maria shook my shoulder. Where was I? Why was I cold and hungry? Then I remembered. The zoo. The gorilla cage. The piano box. I rubbed my eyes.

"Why'd you let me sleep so long?" I asked.

"I fell asleep too," Maria said. "It was boring in here."

"Well, let's go home," I said. "Mom's going to throw a fit."

"We're locked in here, Cody," Maria said. "Not in the gorilla cage. But in the zoo. The main gate's locked. I snuck out and checked while you were asleep."

In the distance, a siren wailed. When it stopped, we could hear tires whisper against concrete on Fifth Avenue. A dog barked. Ordinary daytime sounds are lonesome sounds at night. And smells are stronger. I smelled the musky odor of lion and tiger.

"Maybe we can call a guard," I said. I called but nobody answered. "I think we're stuck here for the night."

"Help! Help!" Maria started to shout.

I put my hand over Maria's mouth. "Shhh, Maria," I said. "Cactus Voice may still be around here. We don't want him to find us. Especially when there's no one else around!"

"You're right," said Maria. It made me feel important to have good ideas.

We sat down to wait. Maria snapped on her radio. We stretched out the headphones so we could both listen. And we turned the volume down low. We listened to country western for a while. Then we heard the news.

"Two children from The Palace Apartments have been reported missing," The announcer said. "Cody Smith and Maria Romero failed to return home this evening. Friends believe the children may be in Central Park. Police have sent search parties to the Ramble." The announcer gave our descriptions. He mentioned our ages. And what we were wearing.

"Maria! They're looking for us," I said. "We'll be rescued."

We took turns peeking through the crack in the box. Surely someone would think to look here. But no one came.

We huddled together to keep warm. I dozed again. Once I heard Maria snoring.

When the sun rose, we woke up. But the zoo gates didn't open for a long time. I didn't tell Maria she snored.

We decided not to call a zookeeper. We'd have to answer too many questions. I wanted to sneak home and give the watches directly to Mom. That seemed like a good idea at first. Then we peeked out.

There stood Cactus Voice. He was waiting at the zoo gate. His eyelids hung at half-mast. I guessed he hadn't had much sleep. He must've been in front of the zoo all night.

"We need to get a zoo worker to help us," Maria said.

"No way," I told her. "Cactus Voice will run. Then

we'll never see him again. Returning the watches won't help much if we lose the thief. Mom's job may depend on that.

"I've got an idea, Maria," I said. "Listen."

"I'm listening," Maria said.

"About midmorning we'll leave the watches here," I said. "We'll sneak out from the zoo one at a time. And in disguise."

"But we don't have a disguise," Maria said.

"People are looking for a boy in old jeans and shirt. They're looking for a girl with long hair. And wearing a brown shirt and new jeans," I explained. "We can change a lot of that."

"How?" Maria asked.

"First, braid your hair," I told her. "That'll make you look different. Then you can wear my shirt over yours. And roll your jeans to the knee. Nobody's going to be watching for just one girl in pigtails. Especially not one wearing a blue shirt and rolled jeans."

"It might work," Maria said.

"I can slip out with no shirt at all," I said. "I'll rip my old jeans into cutoff shorts."

I gave my shirt to Maria. We both worked on our jeans. Then Maria braided her hair. We ripped my shirttail to get strips of cloth to tie her braids.

By the time we were in disguise, the zoo gates had opened. The crowd that had been waiting outside rushed in.

"Now's our chance," Maria said. "Who's first?"

"I'll go first," I said. "But I'm not going to face Mom first. I'll wait for you in the lobby. I'll hide behind the orange vase."

I waited until a large crowd formed inside the zoo. Then luck was with me. The balloon vendor arrived. He stood right in front of the bench where Cactus Voice was sitting. His balloons danced like giant lollipops just above his head.

"So long, Maria. See ya," I said. I eased from the gorilla cage without attracting attention. I was forcing myself to move slowly.

I strolled through the crowd. I kept the balloon vendor between Cactus Voice and me until I was through the zoo entrance.

Then I ran.

I looked over my shoulder once. Nobody was following me. So I slowed to a walk. My heart pounded even after I entered The Palace. I dropped behind the orange vase to rest.

It seemed like hours before Maria arrived. Then suddenly she appeared and nudged me.

"Cody. Come on," Maria said. "Let's get upstairs."

"Maria! I didn't hear you come in. Am I ever glad to see you," I said. I stood up. "We fooled Cactus Voice, didn't we?"

"Yeah. He's still sitting there on the bench," Maria

said. "That balloon man did us a real favor. Are we going up on the elevator?"

"Sure," I said. "I want to tell Spike and Mr. Slovnick everything."

Maria punched the button. The elevator door opened. Mr. Slovnick stood at the controls. He did a double take when he saw us.

Then he ran us to the sixteenth floor and back to our floor. That gave us plenty of time to tell our story. We swore him to silence because we knew we could trust him.

"Some big time you've had," Mr. Slovnick said. "But I don't envy you now. You've a lot of explaining to do. Everyone thinks something terrible has happened to you."

"But we're fine," Maria said.

"Nobody knows that but you. And me," Mr. Slovnick added. "I should have taken you to Cody's mother right off. Curiosity just got the best of me, I guess."

Mr. Slovnick opened the elevator door on our floor. Just then a policeman stepped into the hall. Caterpillar. His uniform looked wrinkled. But his mustache was perky as ever.

"Hey, you kids!" he shouted.

9

A Lie Backfires

"Cody! Maria! We've been frantic!" Mom grabbed us and smothered us with hugs and kisses. She was wearing her own hair. I was really glad to see her.

"Let's get inside," Caterpillar said. "We need privacy."

We went into our apartment. And there stood Mrs. Sugarman in her purple jumpsuit. And, of course, she was ready to serve cake. She laid down her knife long enough to give Maria and me a hug too.

"I just knew you'd be back, safe and sound," Mrs. Sugarman said. "And I knew you'd need food. Nothing like orange cake to give you instant energy."

"No cake yet," Caterpillar said. "I have questions for these kids."

Mrs. Sugarman blinked real fast. Then she left in a huff.

When I was little, I used to think a *huff* was a wagon. Or maybe an old car. I was disappointed when I found out about huffs. But anyway, Mrs. Sugarman left in one this morning.

Caterpillar pulled out his notebook and looked down at us. He reminded me of a hungry owl staring at field mice. But I've never really seen an owl. Or field mice. New York City is short on that kind of wildlife.

"Suppose you kids tell me where you've been and why," Caterpillar said.

"We went to the park to look for Bigfoot," I said. I stalled. I didn't want to spoil things for Mom by telling about the watches.

"Then what?" Caterpillar asked.

"We ducked into a willow thicket," I said.

"And beyond the willows, we found a hollow tree," Maria said. "We thought Bigfoot might be hiding inside it."

"And was he?" Caterpillar asked.

I hated Caterpillar's tone. Flat as a squashed bug. He was making fun of us for looking.

"There wasn't anything inside the hollow tree," I said before Maria could butt in again. "But we saw three big footprints. This long." I held my hands apart to show the length.

"So we knew Bigfoot was around somewhere," Maria said, "and we wanted to get a picture of him."

"Very brave of you." Caterpillar used his squashed-bug voice again. "I suppose you weren't afraid."

"I was," I said. "But we decided to wait and see if he showed up again."

"And you waited in the park all night? Even though you must have known your mother was worrying?" Caterpillar asked.

I gulped and crossed my fingers. "Yes, we waited all night for Bigfoot to show up. But he didn't. So we came on home," I said.

Caterpillar glared at us. "Mrs. Smith, this is no longer a police matter. The kids are back safely. There seems to have been a breakdown in family discipline," he said. "I'll let you handle that. If you'll excuse me, I'll be on my way."

Mom apologized to Caterpillar as he left the apartment. Then she turned to us. "You're going to be punished, of course," she said.

"Wait, Mom," I said. I stood up. "We've got a surprise for you. I couldn't blurt it out in front of Caterpillar—Officer O'Rourke. We found the stolen watches. A whole box of them!

"We can take you to a boy who's mixed up in stealing them. We couldn't tell you in front of Caterpillar. We want you to get credit for finding the watches. Not us. You need the fame, Mom. It'll help you keep your job," I said.

"Slow down and make sense," Mom said. "What's this about stolen watches?"

Maria and I took turns telling the truth about our adventure in the park. Mom wasn't nearly as happy as we had hoped she'd be. In fact, she wasn't happy at all.

"You could have been hurt," Mom shouted.

"But we're safe," I said. "Nothing bad happened. If you don't count spending the night inside a gorilla cage."

"You can return the watches," Maria told Mom. "And make brownie points with your boss."

"Maybe you'll get a raise," I added. I thought that might improve Mom's mood.

Mom put an arm around each of us. But her mouth still quirked. "Cody, we have to call Officer O'Rourke back," she said. "You and Maria must tell him the true story."

"But then he'll know we found the watches. Not you," I said.

"Right," Mom said. She dialed the police. I noticed that she knew the number by heart.

After she hung up, she said, "It'll be a few minutes. His superior will send him back when he gets in. We'll all go to the zoo. And we'll straighten out this matter about the watches."

Maria sighed. I felt sick.

Mom made us bathe and change clothes. I was happy to get rid of my gorilla smell.

Then we went to the lobby to wait. We only waited a few minutes before Caterpillar arrived. He wasn't smiling.

Mom made me tell Caterpillar the true story. I made it clear that we had only lied to help Mom keep her job. Caterpillar just grunted. He didn't smile at all. My neck itched. But I was afraid to scratch.

"The squad car's outside," Caterpillar said at last. "Let's go. I'll tell you my plan on the way to the zoo."

I got to ride up front in between the officers, and Maria sat in back with Mom. I felt sort of important sitting up front that way. But mostly I felt just plain scared.

"Now here's what we're going to do," Caterpillar said at last. "You say the thief was sitting on a bench near the zoo gate, right?"

I nodded.

"Officer Bailey will enter the zoo area first—on foot," Caterpillar said. "He'll keep out of the suspect's sight. He'll pretend to mix with the crowd. Mrs. Smith, you'll follow directly behind Maria, Cody, and me."

"What are Maria and I going to do?" I asked. My

mouth felt dry as cotton.

"I'll walk between you two kids," Caterpillar said. "You can point out the boy. Then we'll make a direct approach toward the suspect. I think he'll run when he sees you two with an officer. I've alerted more men to help Officer Bailey make the arrest.

"I'm glad you've given up your disguises," Caterpillar said. "I feel sure the suspect will recognize you."

"What about the watches?" I asked.

"Once we have the suspect in custody, we'll pick up the watches," Caterpillar said. He looked at Officer Bailey. "Park anywhere along here."

Officer Bailey parked the squad car. And we all got out. I knew how a snail must feel when it crawls out of its shell—very exposed. We saw Cactus Voice still sitting on the bench. I didn't mind a bit when Caterpillar took hold of my hand.

10

Some Thoughts
About Fame

We were half a block from Cactus Voice when he spotted us. He took off running just as Caterpillar had guessed. He zigzagged through the crowd. But Officer Bailey soon caught him.

Three officers surrounded Cactus Voice. They hustled him into another squad car. That was the last we saw of him.

"Kids!" Caterpillar muttered, shaking his head. "Okay, let's get those watches."

Maria and I led him to the gorilla cage. He flashed his badge at the zoo worker. Then we stepped into the cage. I picked up the box of watches and gave it to Caterpillar. He opened it. Probably to make sure I wasn't lying.

"Good work, Cody," he said. "You kids helped us get these young shoplifters."

Maria and I grinned, feeling pleased. Caterpillar returned us to The Palace. After he left, Mom spoke.

"I want you two to eat before I return to work," she said. "Then I want you to stay inside this building for the rest of the day. You can sleep. You can read. You can watch TV. But you aren't to leave the building."

We didn't argue. A day inside The Palace wasn't the end of the world. I felt hungry and sleepy. And I was eager to tell Mr. Slovnick our story.

On floor ten, Mrs. Sugarman met us at her door. She had a meal waiting for us. With cake, of course.

Mom told Mrs. Sugarman our story. And we didn't interrupt. We were eager to get away and tell the same story to Spike.

In spite of the excitement, I had been thinking a lot about my dad. And about being famous. My name would be in the paper again. Somehow I didn't care whether Dad saw it. He didn't care about me. Or he would have called after the first picture appeared.

I felt a little sorry for Dad. I wasn't a nothing. I wasn't a zero. I couldn't expect to have exciting adventures every day, of course. But if another adventure presented itself, I knew I could handle it.

Maybe Dad was the one with the big problem. And not me at all.

We promised Mom to stay inside. As soon as she left, we headed for the elevator. But Mr. Slovnick had passengers. We took the stairs to the basement so we could talk to Spike. I inhaled the musty air. I imagined that it tasted like cobwebs. When we knocked on Spike's door, he didn't answer.

I knocked again. I knocked so hard the door creaked open. A draft blew through the doorway, opening the door farther. That's when Maria and I saw it.

"Cody!" Maria grabbed my wrist. I looked where she was looking. And I saw the Bigfoot costume. It lay crumpled on a couch right inside the doorway. Beside it lay a wooden mold shaped like a giant foot.

"Maria," I whispered. "Spike Slovnick is Bigfoot." My throat felt tight. I was so disappointed. No world record Band-Aid. And now no Bigfoot picture.

And we couldn't turn Spike in to the police. He was our friend.

Now I began to think back. "Maria, remember how

64

Spike came down to his room that first time? The first time we went to the park in the squad car?" I asked.

Maria nodded. "He had plenty of time to call a reporter," she said. "And he was always on hand when pictures were taken. I noticed that."

"Now I remember him almost shoving me into the Bigfoot footprint," I said. "He must've been afraid I wouldn't notice it. Spike! How could he have done this to us!"

"And why?" Maria asked. We stood staring at the evidence until we heard steps on the stairs. We slipped into the hall. And we hid behind some trash cans.

Spike stepped inside his room. Then in a moment he was back. We knew we hadn't left things as they were. He knew someone had snooped.

"Cody? Maria? Are you kids down here?" Spike called.

I was kind of scared. But it was just Spike. So I stepped into sight. So did Maria. At first nobody spoke.

"You saw my Bigfoot outfit, right?" Spike asked at last.

"Yes," I said. "We didn't mean to snoop. We just came to tell you about stuff that's happened."

Maria took over the story. I guess neither of us wanted to ask about the Bigfoot costume. But Spike mentioned it himself.

"What a bummer," Spike said. "I'm just glad you

guys weren't hurt. It would've been my fault." He shook his head.

"You know how it feels not to belong anywhere?" Spike continued. "I mean, I have no friends. I don't fit in at school. None of the guys are interested in plants or birds or nature things. Took me all year to find a buddy."

"Who?" I asked.

"Name's Red Louden," Spike said. "He leads a gang called the Hawks. Guess he noticed me because I always carried a bird book. I wanted to join the Hawks. But to join, a guy has to pass a test. He has to do something that alerts the cops. And he has to face them without getting busted."

"So you did the Bigfoot act," I said.

"Right," said Spike. "I passed the Hawks' test without harming anyone. And I won some publicity too. My business picked up. I grabbed a little attention for Spike Slovnick, Houseplant Consultant."

"But what about the Bigfoot hair we found?" I asked.

"The police lab called back. Turns out it was just a tuft of hair from an Irish setter," Spike said.

"The funny thing is," Spike began, "I really don't care much for the Hawks. They're into spray painting in the subways. That's not my thing."

Spike stopped talking and looked at us. "You going to blab to everyone about what I've done?" he asked.

Suddenly I felt sorry for Spike. I knew what it felt

like to not fit in. But I had an idea. I whispered my idea to Maria. She grinned and agreed to go along with it.

"Spike," I said. "Let's make a deal." I told him about the bird-watchers who needed more leaders. "You know a lot about birds, Spike. And you could study and learn more. Maybe you could lead a bird-watchers group. And really help those museum people a lot."

"In a job like that, you'd meet people who might need a houseplant consultant," Maria said.

"Maria and I won't blab about your Bigfoot caper if you'll go to the museum," I said. "Ask about a part-time job."

"They'll turn me down cold," Spike said.

"Just try for it," I said. "Maybe Mr. Slovnick will go with you. I think they'll listen to a recommendation from a retired science teacher. Will you try it, Spike?"

"I don't have much choice, do I?" Spike said. "If you blab about Bigfoot, I might get kicked out of this place."

Maria and I wouldn't blab anyway. But I didn't let on to Spike. This could be his big chance.

"I'll try for it, kids," Spike said. "I'm glad you guys understand. I guess I've got friends after all. And maybe I do belong. Right here at The Palace."

"Spike, will you help me make another wren house? Maybe tomorrow after I've had some sleep?" I asked.

"Sure, Cody," Spike said.

"All those bird-watchers need birds to watch, don't they? And wrens need houses. Why, I'm going to be like Johnny Appleseed. Only instead of planting apple seeds, I'll hang wren houses," I said.

"Cody Wrenhouse!" Maria laughed.

"It's not funny, Maria. You'll stop laughing when I make the *Guinness Book*," I said. "You won't laugh when I become a very famous person. I intend to do that this summer."

But I laughed too. It would be fun to try to be famous for doing something useful. Who cared about wearing a Band-Aid? Who cared about finding Bigfoot?

"You got that Band-Aid on again?" Maria asked me.

"Nope," I said, grinning. "But I think the *Guinness* people will still write me up. They'll respect the first person to hang 100 wren houses in Central Park!"